The Giant Jam Sandwich

First published 1972 by Jonathan Cape Limited
First published in paperback 1974 by Pan Books Limited
This revised edition published 2009 by Macmillan Children's Books
a division of Macmillan Publishers Limited
20 New Wharf Road, London N1 9RR
Basingstoke and Oxford
Associated companies throughout the world
Published in association with Jonathan Cape Limited
www.panmacmillan.com

ISBN: 978-0-330-50742-4

3 5 7 9 10 8 6 4

A CIP catalogue record for this book is available from the British Library

Printed in Belgium

The Giant JAM Sandwich

STORY AND PICTURES BY

John Vernon Lord

WITH VERSES BY

Janet Burroway

Macmillan Children's Books in association with Jonathan Cape

For Alexander and Jonathan

One hot summer in Itching Down,
Four million wasps flew into town.

They drove the picnickers away,   They chased the farmers from their hay,

They stung Lord Swell on his fat bald pate,   They dived and hummed and buzzed and ate,

And the noisy, nasty nuisance grew
Till the villagers cried, "What *can* we *do?*"

So they called a meeting in the village hall,
And Mayor Muddlenut asked them all,
"What *can* we *do?*" And they said, "Good question!"
But nobody had a good suggestion.

Then Bap the Baker leaped to his feet
And cried,"What do wasps like best to eat?
Strawberry jam! Now wait a minute!
If we made a giant sandwich we could trap them in it!"

The gentlemen cheered, the ladies squealed,
And Farmer Seed said, "Use my field."

Bap gave instructions for the making of the dough.
"Mix flour from above and yeast from below.
Salt from the seaside, water from the spout.
Now thump it! Bump it! Bang it about!"

While they were working, and working hard,
Some more made a tablecloth out in the yard.

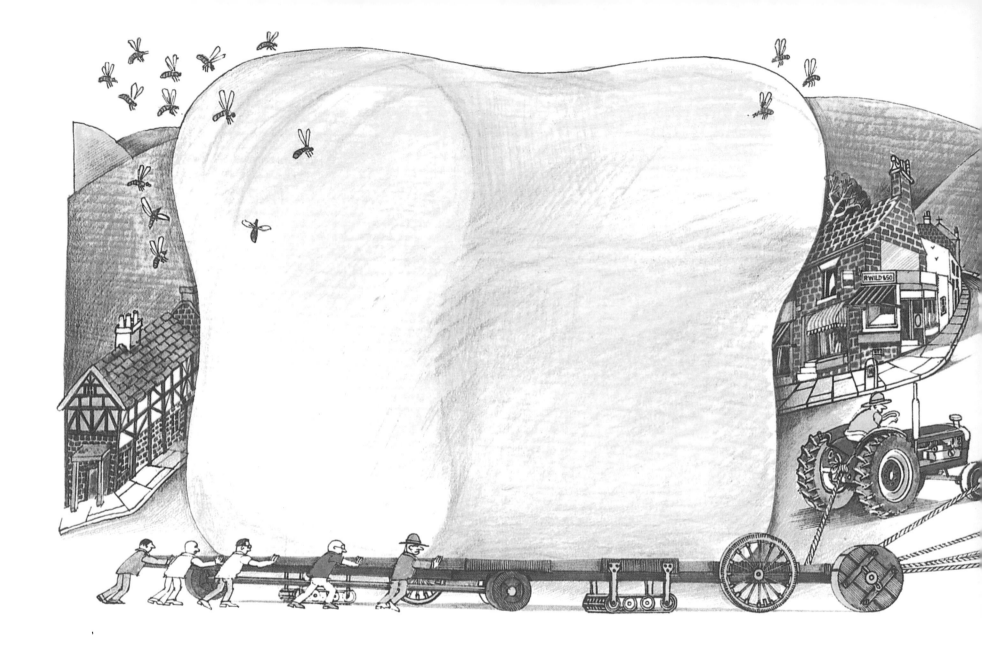

When they were done, the dough was left to rise
Till the loaf was a mountain in shape and size!

They hitched it up, with a bit of fuss,
To tractors, cars and the village bus,
And took it to the oven they had made on the hill –
Fifty cookers in an old brick mill.

For hours and hours they let it cook.
It swelled inside till the windows shook.

It was piping hot when they took it out,
And the villagers raised a mighty shout.

"Isn't it crusty! Aren't we clever!"   But the wasps were just as bad as ever.

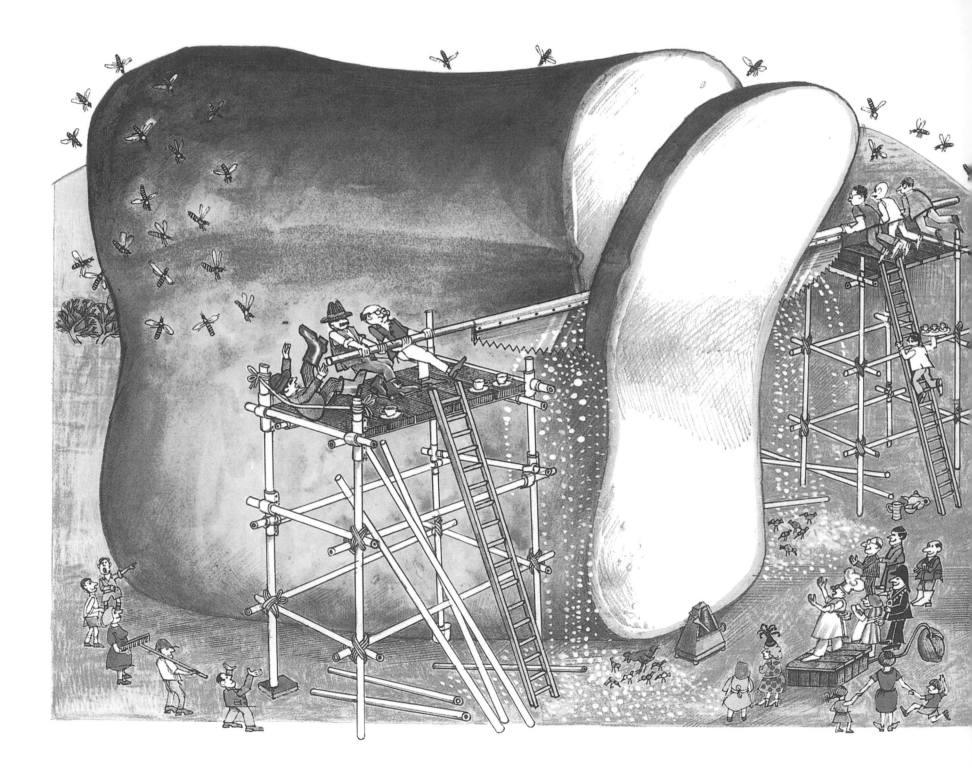

The loaf was left to cool, and then
The people watched while six strong men
Took a great big saw and sliced right through.
Everybody clapped, and they cut slice two.

The village bus, they all agreed,
Would spoil the fields of Farmer Seed,
So eight fine horses pulled the bread
To where the picnic cloth was spread.

A truck drew up and dumped out butter,
And they spread it out with a flap and a flutter.
Spoons and spades! Slap and slam!
And they did the same with the strawberry jam.

Meanwhile, high above the field,
Six flying machines whirred and wheeled,
Ready for the wasps to take the bait.
And then there was nothing to do but wait.

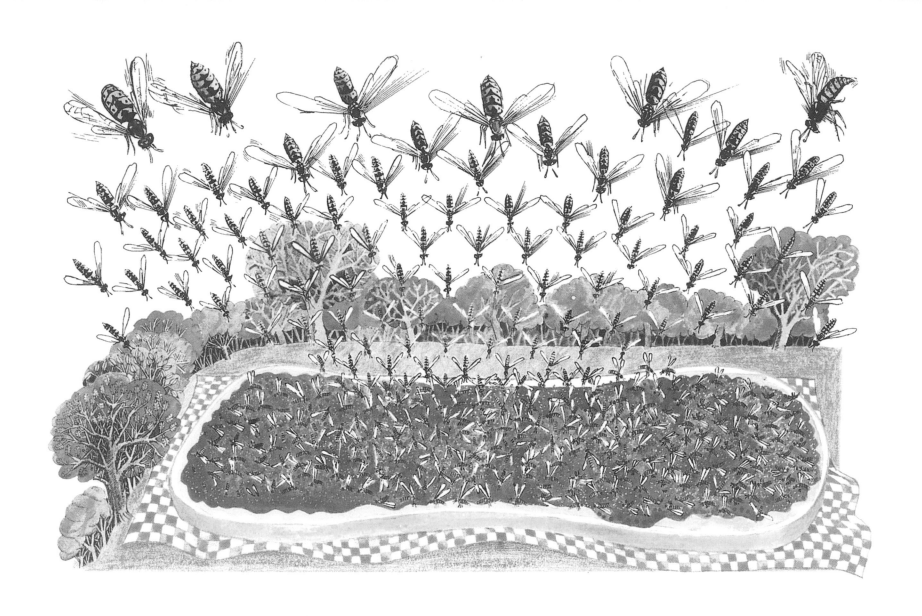

Suddenly the sky was humming!
All four million wasps were coming!
They smelled that jam, they dived and struck!
And they ate so much that they all got stuck.

The other slice came down – kersplat! –
On top of the wasps, and that was that.
There were only three that got away,
And where they are now I cannot say.

But they never came back to Itching Down,
Which is not a waspish sort of town,
But a very nice place to dance and play.
And that's what the villagers did that day.

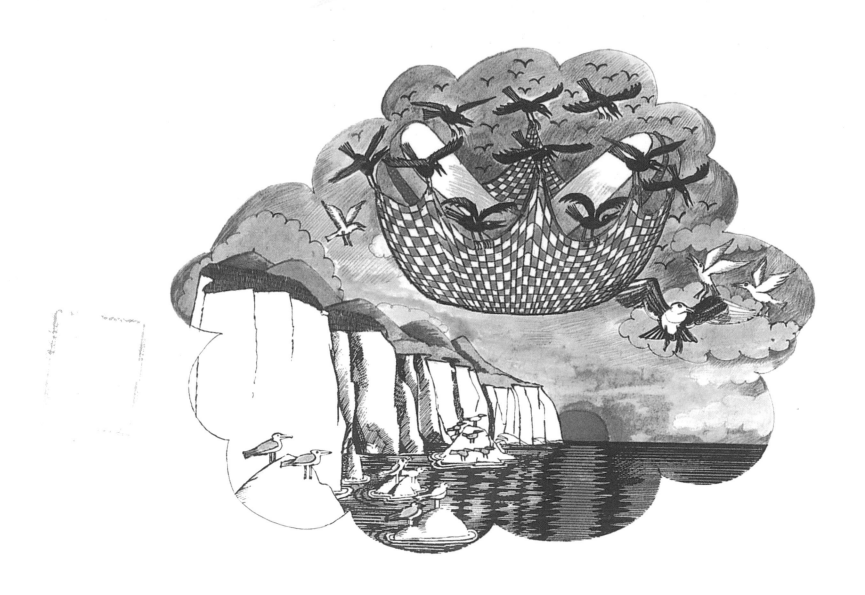

What became of the sandwich? Well,
In Itching Down they like to tell
How the birds flew off with it in their beaks
And had a feast for a hundred weeks.